MRS FOX

Sarah Hall was born in Cumbria in 1974. She is the author of four novels, *Haweswater*, *The Electric Michelangelo*, *The Carhullan Army* and *How to Paint a Dead Man*, and winner of the Commonwealth Writers' Prize, the Betty Trask Award, the John Llewellyn Rhys Prize and the Portico Prize. *The Electric Michelangelo* was also shortlisted for the Man Booker Prize and longlisted for the Orange Prize.

The Beautiful Indifference, her collection of short stories, won the Edge Hill Prize and Reader's Award, and was shortlisted for the Frank O'Connor International Short Story Award. The first story in the collection, 'Butchers Perfume', was shortlisted for the BBC National Short Story Award, a prize she won in 2013 with 'Mrs Fox', a story inspired by David Garnett's 1922 novella *Lady Into Fox*.

MRS FOX

Sarah Hall

FABER & FABER

First published in 2014
by Faber & Faber Limited
Bloomsbury House
74–77 Great Russell Street, London WC1B 3DA

Typeset by Faber
Printed in England by CPI Group (UK) Ltd, Croydon, CRO 4YY

A CIP record for this book
is available from the British Library

ISBN 978–0–571–31567–3

2 4 6 8 10 9 7 5 3 1

For Lucy and Tom

THAT HE LOVES HIS WIFE is unquestionable. All day at work he looks forward to seeing her. On the train home, he reads, glancing up at the stations of commuter towns, land-steal under construction, slabs of mineral-looking earth, and pluming clouds. He imagines her robe falling as she steps across the bedroom. Usually he arrives first, while she drives back from her office. He pours a drink and reclines on the sofa. When the front door opens he rouses. He tries to wait, for her to come and find him, and tell him about her day, but he hasn't the patience. She is in the kitchen, taking her coat off, unfastening her shoes. Her form, her essence, a scent of corrupted rose.

–Hello, darling, she says.

The shape of her eyes, almost Persian,

though she is English. Her waist and hips in the blue skirt; he watches her move – to the sink, to the table, to the chair where she sits, slowly, with a woman's grace. Under the hollow of her throat, below the collar of her blouse, is a dribble of fine gold, a chain, on which hangs her wedding ring.

–Hello, you.

He bends to kiss her, his hands in his pockets. Such simple pleasure; she is his to kiss.

He, or she, cooks; this is the modern world, both of them are capable, both busy. They eat dinner, sometimes they drink wine. They talk or listen to music; nothing in particular. There are no children yet.

Later, they move upstairs and prepare for bed. He washes his face, urinates. He likes to leave the day on his body. He wears nothing to sleep in; neither does his wife, but she has showered, her hair is damp, darkened to wheat. Her skin is incredibly soft; there is no corrugation on her rump. Her pubic hair is harsh when it dries; it crackles against his palm, contrasts strangely with what's inside. A mystery he wants to solve every night.

2

There are positions they favour, that feel and make them appear unusual to each other. The trick is to remain slightly detached. The trick is to be able to bite, to speak in a voice not your own. Afterwards, she goes to the bathroom, attends to herself, and comes back to bed. His sleep is blissful, dreamless.

Of course, this is not the truth. No man is entirely contented. He has stray erotic thoughts, and irritations. She is slow to pay bills. She is messy in the bathroom; he picks up bundles of wet towels every day. Occasionally, he uses pornography, if he is away for work. He fantasizes about other women, some of whom look like old girlfriends, some like his wife. If a woman at work or on the train arouses him, he wonders about the alternative, a replacement. But in the wake of these moments, he suffers vertiginous fear, imagines losing her, and he understands what she means. It is its absence which defines the importance of a thing.

And what of this wife? She is in part unknowable, as all clever women are. The marrow is adaptable, which is not to say she is guileful, just that she will survive. Only once has she been unfaithful. She is desirable, but to elicit adoration there must be more than sexual qualities. Something in her childhood has made her withheld. She makes no romantic claims, does not require reassurance, and he adores her because of the lack. The one who loves less is always loved more. After she has cleaned herself and joined him in bed, she dreams subterranean dreams, of forests, dark corridors and burrows, roots and earth. In her purse, alongside the makeup and money, is a small purple ball. A useless item, but she keeps it – who can say why? She is called Sophia.

Their house is modern, in a town in the corona of the city. Its colours are arable: brassica, taupe, flax. True angles, long surfaces, invisible, soft-closing drawers. The mortgage is large. They have invested in bricks, in the concept of home. A cleaner comes on Thursdays. There are similar houses nearby, newly built along the edgelands, in the lesser countryside – what was once heath.

4

One morning he wakes to find his wife vomiting into the toilet. She is kneeling, retching, but nothing is coming up. She is holding the bowl. As she leans forward the notches in her spine rise against the flesh of her back. Her protruding bones, the wide-open mouth, a clicking sound in her gullet: the scene is disconcerting, his wife is almost never ill. He touches her shoulder.

–Are you all right? Can I do anything?

She turns. Her eyes are bright, the brightness of fever. There is a coppery gleam under her skin. She shakes her head. Whatever is rising in her has passed. She closes the lid, flushes, and stands. She leans over the sink and drinks from the tap, not sips, but long sucks of water. She dries her mouth on a towel.

–I'm fine.

She lays a hand, briefly, on his chest, then moves past him into the bedroom. She begins to dress, zips up her skirt, fits her heels into the backs of her shoes.

–I won't have breakfast. I'll get something later. See you tonight.

She kisses him goodbye. Her breath is slightly sour. He hears the front door slam and the car engine start. His wife has a strong constitution. She does not often take to her bed. In the year they met she had some kind of mass removed, through an opened abdomen; she got up and walked the hospital corridors the same day. He goes into the kitchen and cooks an egg. Then he too leaves for work.

Later, he will wonder, and through the day he worries. But that evening, when they return to the house, will herald only good things. She seems well again, radiant even, having signed a new contract at work for the sale of a block of satellite offices. The greenish hue to her skin is gone. Her hair is undone and all about her shoulders. She pulls him forward by his tie.

–Thank you for being so sweet this morning.

They kiss. He feels relief, but over what he's not sure. He untucks her blouse, slips his fingers under the waistband of her skirt. She indicates her willingness. They move upstairs and reduce each other to nakedness. He bends before her. A wide badge of hair, undepilated, spreads at the top of her thighs. The taste reminds him of a river. They take longer than usual. He is strung between immense climactic pleasure and delay. She does not come, but she is ardent; finally he cannot hold back.

They eat late – cereal in bed – spilling milk from the edges of the bowls, like children. They laugh at the small domestic adventure; it's as if they have just met.

Tomorrow is the weekend, when time becomes luxurious. But his wife does not sleep late, as she usually would. When he wakes she is already up, in the bathroom. There is the sound of running water, and under its flow another sound, the low cry of someone expressing injury, a burn, or a cut, a cry like a bird, but wider of throat. Once, twice, he hears it. Is she sick again? He knocks on the door.

–Sophia?

She doesn't answer. She is a private woman; this is her business. Perhaps she is fighting a flu. He goes to the kitchen to make coffee. Soon she joins him. She has bathed and dressed but does not look well. Her face is pinched, dark around the eye sockets, markedly so, as if an overnight gauntening has taken place.

–Oh, poor you, he says. What would you like to do today? We could stay here and take it easy, if you don't feel well.

–Walk, she says. I'd like some air.

He makes toast for her but she takes only a bite or two. He notices that the last chewed mouthful has been put back on her plate, a damp little brown pile. She keeps looking towards the window.

–Would you like to go for a walk now? he asks.

She nods and stands. At the back door she pulls on leather boots, a coat, a yellow scarf, and moves restlessly while he finds his jacket. They walk through the cul-de-sac, ringed by calluna houses, past the children's play area at the end of the road, the concrete pit with conical mounds where children skate. It is still early; no one is around. Intimations of frost under north-facing gables. Behind the morning mist, a faint October sun has begun its industry. They walk through a gateway onto scrubland, then into diminutive trees, young ash, recently planted around the skirt of the older woods. Two miles away, on the other side of the heath, towards the city, bull-dozers are levelling the earth, extending the road system.

Sophia walks quickly on the dirt path, perhaps trying to walk away the virus, the malaise, whatever it is that's upsetting her system. The path rises and falls, chicanes permissively. There are ferns and grasses, twigs angling up, leaf-spoils, the brittle memory of wild garlic and summer flowers. Towards the centre, a few older trees have survived; their branches heavy, their bark flaking, trunks starred with orange lichen. Birds dip and dart between bushes. The light breaks through; a gilded light, terrestrial but somehow holy. She moves ahead. They do not speak, but it is not uncompanionable. He allows himself, for a few moments, to be troubled by irrational thoughts – she has a rapid, senseless cancer and will waste, there will be unconscionable pain, he will hold a fatal vigil beside her bed. Outliving her will be dire. Her memory will be like a wound in him. But, as he watches her stride in front, he can see that she is fit and healthy. Her body swings, full of energy. What is it then? An unhappiness? A confliction? He dares not ask.

The woods begin to thicken: oak and beech. A jay flaps across the thicket, lands on the ground nearby; he admires the primary blue elbow before it flutters off. Sophia turns her head sharply in the direction of its flight. She picks up her pace and begins to walk strangely on the tips of her toes, her knees bent, her heels lifted. Then she leans forward and in a keen, awkward position begins to run. She runs hard. Her feet toss up fragments of turf and flares of leaves. Her hair gleams – the chromic sun renders it livid. She runs, at full tilt, as if pursued.

–Hey, he calls. Hey! Stop! Where are you going?

Fifty yards away, she slows and stops. She

crouches on the path as he hurries after her, her body twitching in an effort to remain still. He catches up.

–What was all that about! Darling?

She turns her head and smiles. Something is wrong with her face. The bones have been recarved. Her lips are thin and her nose is a dark blade. Teeth small and yellow. The lashes of her hazel eyes have thickened and her brows are drawn together, an expression he has never seen, a look that is almost craven. A trick of kiltering light on this English autumn morning. The deep cast of shadows from the canopy. He blinks. She turns to face the forest again. She is leaning forward, putting her hands down, lifting her bottom. She has stepped out of her laced boots and is walking away. Now she is running again, on all fours, lower to earth, sleeker, fleeter. She is running and becoming smaller, running and becoming smaller, running in the light of the reddening sun, the red of her hair and her coat falling, the red of her fur and her body loosening. Running. Holding behind her a sudden, brazen object, white-tipped. Her yellow scarf trails in the briar. All vestiges shed. She stops, within calling distance, were he not struck dumb. She looks over her shoulder. Topaz eyes glinting. Scorched face. Vixen.

October light, no less duplicitous than any season's. Bird calls. Plants shriveling. The moon, palely bent on the horizon, is setting. Everything, swift or slow, continues. He looks at the fox on the path in front of him. Any moment, his wife will walk between the bushes. She will crawl out of the wen of woven ferns. The undergrowth, which must surely have taken her, will yield her. *How amazing,* she'll whisper, pointing up the track. These are his thoughts, standing in the morning sun, staring, and wrestling belief. Insects pass from stalk to stalk. The breeze through the trees is sibilant.

On the path, looking back at him, is a brilliant creature, which does not move, does not flinch or sidle off. No. She turns fully and hoists the tail around beside her like a flaming sceptre. Slim limbs and slender nose. A badge of white from jaw to breast. Her head thrust low and forward, as if she is looking along the earth into the future. His mind's a shock of useless thought, denying, hectoring, until one lone voice proceeds through the chaos. *You saw, you saw, you saw.* He says half words, nothing sensible. And now she trots towards him down the path, as a dog would, returning to its master.

Nerve and instinct. Her thousand feral programs. Should she not flee into the borders, kicking away the manmade world? She comes to him, her coy, sporting body held on elegant black-socked legs. A moment ago: Sophia. He stands still. His mind stops exchanging. At his feet, she sits, her tail rearing. Exceptional, winged ears. Eyes like the spectrum of her blended fur. He kneels, and with absolute tenderness, touches the ruff of her neck, which would be soft, were it not for the light tallowing of hairs.

What can be decided in a few moments that will not be questioned for a lifetime? He collects her coat from the nearby bushes. He moves to place it, gently, around her – she does not resist – and, his arms reaching cautiously under, he lifts her. The moderate weight of a mid-sized mammal. The scent of musk, gland, and faintly, faintly, her perfume – a dirty rose.

And still, in the woods and on the apron of grassland, no one is hiking, though soon there will be dogs tugging against leads, old couples, children gadding about. Down the path he walks, holding his fox. Her brightness escapes the coat at both ends; it is like trying to wrap fire. Her warmth against his chest is astonishing – for a wife who always felt the cold, in her hands and feet. She is calm; she does not struggle, and he bears her like a sacrifice, a forest pieta.

Half a mile in secret view. Past the sapling ash trees, through the heath gate, past the concrete pit where one sole girl is turning tricks on her board, practising before the boys come, her gaze held down over the front wheels. There are the houses – new builds, each spanking, chimneyless, their garages closed – and he must walk the gauntlet of suburbia, his heart founding a terrible rhythm at the thought of doors opening,

14

blinds being lifted, exposure. Somewhere nearby a car door slams. She shifts in his arms and his grip tightens. Around the bend; he ignores the distracted neighbour who is moving a bin. Up the pathway to number 34. She is heavier now, deadening his muscles. He moves her to the crux of his left arm, reaches into his trouser pocket for the keys, fumbles, drops them, bends down. She, thinking he is releasing her perhaps, begins to wriggle and scramble towards the ground, but he keeps her held in his aching arm, he lifts the keys from the flagstones, opens the door and enters. He closes the door behind and all the world is shut out.

Suddenly his rescuer's strength goes. His arms give. Sensing it, she jumps, her back claws raking his forearm. She lands sheerly on the carpet. She holds still a second or two, shakes, then goes into the kitchen, directly, no investigation of location, and jumps onto a chair next to the table. As if only now, after her walk and purging of the disease of being human, she is ready for breakfast.

*

These first hours with his new wife pass, not in wonderment, nor in confusion or fugue, but a kind of acute discerning. She positions herself in the house, wherever she fancies, as she might otherwise have. He follows, making sure she has not vanished, making sure he is conscious. The spectacular evidence remains. He is able to approach. He is able to touch the back of her head, under the slim, almost bearded jaw, even the pads of her paws, which are so sensitive her flesh quivers. Like a curious lover he studies her form. The remarkable pelt, forged as if in a crucible of ruddy, igneous landscapes. The claws that have left long angry scratches on his arm: crescent-shaped, blond and black. The triangular, white-lined ears, with tall, dark guard hairs. The bend in her hind legs; the full, shapely thighs, similar, in a way, to a woman squatting. He studies sections, details. Her eyes, up close, are the colour of the Edwardian citrine brooch he bought her for her birthday.

He speaks quietly, says things she might want to hear, consolations. *I am sorry. It will be all right.* The day is lost. For much of it she sleeps. She sleeps curled on the floor. Her ribs palpitate. As dusk arrives he tries to eat, but can't. He picks her up and carries her to the bed. She repositions and closes her eyes again. Gently, he lies down next to her. He puts a hand to her side, where she is reddest. The texture of her belly is smooth and delicate, like scar tissue; small nubbed teats under the fur. Her smell is gamey; smoky, sexual.

–Sophia, he whispers, don't worry, though she is not, as far as he can tell, distressed.

He closes his eyes. Sleep, the cure for all catastrophes, will bring relief, perhaps even reversal.

When he wakes there is the faint lunar bloom of streetlight in the bedroom and she is gone. He starts up. He moves through the house, desperately, like a man searching for a bomb. No dream could ever be so convincing. He rushes downstairs, and at the bottom treads in something slightly crusted and yielding. Quickly, he searches on. He calls out her name, feeling ever more its falseness.

She is standing on the kitchen table, an unmistakable silhouette, cut from the wild. She is looking out of the French windows at the garden, the nocturnal world. She is seeing what alien sights? The fresnel lenses of owl's eyes, luminous grassy trails, or bats blurting across the lawn? The grisly aroma of what he has trodden in rises to his nose. He wipes his foot on the carpet. He sits at the table and puts his head in his hands. She watches the garden.

Sunday. Monday. He fields phone calls from his and her places of work. He manages to lie convincingly, asks for personal leave. There is no milk. He drinks black tea. He eats cold soup, a stump of staling bread. He puts down bowls of water on the kitchen floor, but either she does not like the purity or the chlorine. He sits for hours, thinking, silent – every time he speaks he feels the stupidity of words. What has happened? Why? He is not able to unlock anything reasonable in his mind. She is in the house, a bright mass, a beautiful arch being, but he feels increasingly alone. He does not let her out, cruel as it seems, though she pays particular attention to the doors and vents where small drafts of outside air can be felt and smelled – he watches her sniffing the seal, gently clawing the frame. If this does not pass, he thinks, he will take himself to the doctor, or her to the veterinary – one of them will discover the truth, the contraspective madness. But then, how can he?

The sound of a key in the front door lock startles him. He has been lying naked on the bedroom floor while she patrols. It is Esmé, the cleaner. It is Thursday. Nine a.m. He pulls on a robe, dashes down the stairs, and catches her just as she is coming into the hallway, dropping her bag on the floor, the door gaping open behind her.

–No, he shouts. No! Go away. You have to go.

He puts a hand on her shoulder and begins to manoeuvre her backwards, towards the door. She gasps in shock at such treatment. Her employer is never home when she cleans – all she knows of him is the money he leaves on the table, the addressed letters she moves from doormat to counter, and it's his wife who speaks to her on the phone. She barely recognizes him, and for a moment mistakes him for an intruder.

–What? What? Take your hands off. I, I'll –

She is alarmed, he can see, at the blockade, at being handled by a dishevelled, undressed man. He gathers his wits, releases her arm.

–Don't clean this week, Esmé. We have a terrible bug. It's very contagious. I don't want to risk you getting it.

He is pale, a little crazed, but does not look ill.

–Sophia has it?

–Yes. She does.

–Does she need anything? I can go to the pharmacy.

–I'm taking care of her. Thank you. Please –

He gestures for her to leave. Routed, Esmé picks up her bag and steps away. He closes the door behind her, moves to the hall window and watches. She glances up at the bedroom, frowns, walks to her little blue car, gets in, and drives away. When he turns round the fox is standing at the top of the stairs.

Later that day, tense with anxiety, he leaves the house and goes to the library. He researches. *Delusional disorder. Folie à deux. Poison effects.* Then: *Transmogrification. Fables.* If he can avail himself of understanding, reason, definition . . . He returns home with medical texts and a slender yellow volume from the twenties. There is little correlation. He is no thwarted lover. Nor are there other symptoms. Most upsetting is the repetition of one aspect: *an act of will.*

So it continues. He enters a room and at first does not notice that she is up on top of the cabinet, on the windowsill, in the sliding food rack, which he has left open. Her poise so still she is entirely missable, the way all wild things are, until the rustic outline comes into focus. The surprise of seeing her, every time, in proximity; a thing from another realm that he has brought home to belong. She sleeps. She sleeps neatly in a circle, tail tucked under her chin. Not on the bed, where he keeps trying to put her, but on a chair seat, in the corner of the utility room. The house is warm but she makes the most of extra heat wherever she can find it – the sitting place he has just vacated, under the boiler. He cleans away the black, twisted scat that he finds, tries not to be disgusted. *If we were old*, he tells himself, *if I were her carer*. He leaves plates of food on the floor, milk-soaked bread, cooked chicken, inoffensive dishes, which she investigates, tries, but does not finish. Instead she looks up at him, her brows steepling, haughty, unsatisfied. Part of his brain will not translate what she wants: that she must have it raw. Her eyes flicker after birds in the garden. Even trapped behind glass, she calculates. The metrics of the hunt. Hating the humiliation, he brings home a can of dogfood, tips the jellied lump out onto a china dinner plate. She rejects it. He finds her licking her lips and trotting out of the kitchen. On the expensive slate floor is a dark patch of saliva – she has licked something up, a spider perhaps.

He cannot speak to her anymore. She doesn't understand and his voice sounds ridiculous to his own ears, a cacophany. She will not tolerate being in the same room for long. She roams, sniffs at the back door. She wants what's outside, she is becoming restive, growling, but he knows he cannot let her go. What would become of her, and, with her, his hope? He inches around the front door when he leaves and locks it behind, is careful when re-entering the house. He phones and tells the cleaning woman her services are no longer needed.

And he knows; in this terrible arrangement, it is he who is not adjusting; he who is failing their relationship. So he decides. He buys uncooked meat from the butcher, offal, and in a moment of bravado, throws it onto the floor in front of her. She nips at a purple lobe, then walks away. Surely she is hungry! *You are a fool*, he tells himself. The next day he goes to a specialty shop and brings home a live bird. A pigeon. Its wings are clipped. He sets it on the floor, where it hops and tries to lift. Within moments she is beside it, crouching, lit with energy. He watches as she recoils and then pounces high, higher than she need, in excitement or prowess, and comes down hard on the helpless flurrying thing. She bites its iridescent neck. She twists its head. She is like machinery; the snapping and clicking of her teeth. The lavender breast is opened, there are riches inside. He turns and leaves, feeling sickened. He is angry and ashamed. That she could ever, even before this, be his pet.

It cannot go on – the proof is everywhere. Musk on the doorframes. Stains on the carpet. Downy feathers. And his unnatural longing, which can never be resolved, nor intimacy converted, even as his mind nudges against the possibility. Whatever godly or congugal test this is, he has certainly failed. He decides. He opens the utility door and leaves it standing wide. He sits outside it with his back against the cold house wall. In the garden is a muddy, mushroomy smell – tawny November. Under the trees, husks and hard fruits are furling and rotting. He waits. The pressure and temperature of the house changes, scents enter, great free gusts of coppice and bonfire and heath, and beyond, the city's miasma. It doesn't take long. Her head and shoulders come through the doorway. She pauses, one front paw lifted and pointing, her jaws parted, the folded tongue lifting up. He stares straight ahead. *Just go. Please.* He tells himself it is not a choice. He does not want her to leave and yet he can no longer stand the lunacy, the impasse, his daily torment. Sophia has gone, he tells himself.

She bolts, a long streak of russet down the lawn, between the plum trees, and up over the fence, the white tip flashing like an afterthought.

He feels nothing. Not relief. Not sorrow. That night he leaves the back door standing open, love's caveat. In the morning there are slugs and silvery trails on the kitchen floor, sodden leaves blown in, and the bin has been knocked over. The following night he shuts the door, though does not lock it. His dreams are anguished, involving machinery and dogs, his own brutality, and blood.

Winter. A little snow, which gives England an older, calmer appearance. She has not come back. He worries about the cold, what might become of her, out there. There are distant nocturnal screams, like a woman being forced – are they hers? He checks the garden for signs, prints in the crisp skin of ice, her waste. The line he tells is one of simple separation. The neighbours do not ask further questions. A letter arrives from her place of work accepting termination of employment. All the while the enormity of what has happened haunts him. The knowledge might send him mad, he thinks. One day he will take off his clothes and lie in the street and beat his head with his fists and laugh as if choking. He will admit to killing her, beg for jail, though her body will never be found.

He returns to work. He is polite and, to new workers in the office, sullen-seeming. Those who know him, those who met his wife, understand something important has been extinguished. He cannot quite reclaim himself. He feels victimhood strongly. Something has been taken from him. Taken, and in the absurdest possible way. He pities himself, abhors his passivity – could he not have done more? After a while it dawns on him that she doesn't want to come back, that perhaps she did not want what she had. *An act of will.* Her clothes hang in the wardrobe, until, one morning – the mornings are always easier and more decisive – he gathers them up, folds them carefully and places them in bags. He goes through the contents of her purse, which offers no enlightening information, not even her lipstick, a red hue women can rarely wear, or the small purple ball, too gnomic to interpret. But these intimate items he cannot throw away. He places them in a bottom drawer.

Enough, he thinks.

He tries to forget. He tries to masturbate. He thinks of others, of partial, depersonalized images, obscenities; he concentrates, but release will not come. Instead, he weeps.

A week later, close to Christmas, he begins to walk on the heath again. That moulted protean place, which he has for weeks avoided. He walks at first light, when the paths are deserted, and the low red sun glimmers between bare twigs. He is not looking. He is not looking and yet he feels keenly aware of this old, colloquial tract of land, with its debris of nature, hemmed in by roads and houses, lathed away by bulldozers. It is fecund. It is rife with a minority of lifeforms. Black birds in the stark arboretum, larval-looking and half-staged in the uppermost branches. The dead grass rustling. A flash of wing or leg. Sometimes he sits for a while, his collar turned up, his gloveless hands on the fallen trunk, whose sap is hard and radiant. His breath clouds the air. He is here, now. He would give himself, except there is no contract being offered.

He might find comfort in the sinew of winter, when nothing exists but that which is already exposed, and so he does, slowly, and as the earth tilts back towards the sun, his mind begins to ease. To be comfortable inside one's sadness is not valueless. This too will pass. All things tend towards transience, mutability. It is in such mindful moments, when everything is both held and released, that revelation comes.

*

She appears on the path in front of him, in the budding early spring. He has been staring down at his feet as they progress, at the shivering stems and petals. All around him, the spermy smell of blossom. *Yes*, the world is saying, *I begin*. He looks up. The vixen is on a grass mound, twenty feet ahead. She is like a comet in the surroundings, her tail, her flame. She has her head lowered, as if in humility, as if in apology for her splendour, the black backs of her ears visible. Oh, her golden greening eyes! Her certainty of colour! How easily she can fell him; and he will always fall.

She faces him. He waits to hear his name, just his name, that he could be made unmad by it. She steps into the low scrub of the forest floor, takes a few high and tidy steps, and he thinks at first the wilderness has finally untamed her, she is afraid, about to run. But she turns, and pauses. Another step. A backward glance. What then, is she piloting? Is he to follow?

The old, leftover stretch of heath, preserved by a tenuous council ruling, by councillors who dine in expensive restaurants with developers, has a crock of boulders and hardwoods at its centre. Moss. Thrift. Columbine. Tides of lesser vasculars. She picks her way in, a route invisible to his eye, but precisely marked, it seems. Rock to stump, she crosses and criss-crosses. She knows he is following; his footfalls are mortifying, though he tries to tread respectfully through this palace of delicate filaments. He keeps his distance. He must convey at all costs that he has no intention to touch her, take her, or otherwise destroy the accord. The roots of old trees rear out of the ground, pulling strings of soil up with them. These are earnest natives; they have survived blight and lightning and urban expansion. They bear the weight of mythical, hollow thrones. Lungs of fungi hang from their branches.

Beneath one trunk there is an opening, a gash between stones and earth. Her den. She makes a circuit of the nearby copse, then sits beside the entrance, laying her flaring tail alongside her. Her belly is pinkish and swollen. She is thinner than he remembered, her legs long and narrow-footed, like a deer's.

She cocks her head, as if giving him licence to speak. But no, he must not think this way. Nothing of the past is left, except the shadow on his mind. From her slender jaw she produces a low sound, like a chirp, a strangled bark. She repeats it. He does not know what it means. In their house she was never vocal, except with displeasure. Then, from the dark gape, a sorrel cub emerges, its paws tentative on the den-run, its eyes opaque, blueish, until only recently blind, a charcoal vulpine face. Another follows, nudging the first. And another. There are four. They stumble towards their mother. They fit to her abdomen, scrambling for position, stepping on and over each other. As she feeds them her eyes blink closed, sensually, then she stares at him.

Privy to this, no man could be ready. Not at home, skulling the delivery within the bloody sheets, nor in the theatre gown, standing behind a screen as the surgeon extracts the child. Human inhibition is gone. What he sees is the core of purpose. His mind is stupefied. They are, they must be, his. He crouches slowly.

She is thirled to the task, but not impatient. Before they are done she nudges the cubs away. They nose against each other. They rock, vulnerably, on their paws, licking the beads of milk. A great inspirational feeling lets loose in him. He has sweeping masculine thoughts. He understands his duty. He swears silent oaths to himself and to her: that he will guard this secret protectorate. That he will forego all else. He will, if it comes to it, lie down in front of the diggers before they level this shrine.

They remain above ground a moment longer. They play in silence, programmed to safe mutism, while she watches. They have her full attention. Their coats are dirty, sandy camouflage, but nothing will be left to chance. She curtails their crèche. One by one, she lifts them by their scruffs towards the hole, sends them back inside, and then, without hesitating, disappears after.

As he leaves he memorizes the way. The den is not as far from the path as he thought, dogs off their leads will detect their secretions, but it is secluded, lost behind a sward of bracken. She knows. His head is full of gold as he walks home. He allows himself the temporary glow of pride, and then relinquishes. He has no role, except as guest. The truth is their survival is beyond his control.

He does not return every day, but once a week makes an early foray into the woods. He approaches respectfully, remains at a distance; a watcher, estranged. He never catches them out but must wait for an appearance. They materialize from the ground, from the undergrowth, an oak stump. If they know him they show no indication. Past a look or two – their eyes eerie and hazelish – they pay him no heed. Their mother has sanctioned his presence, that is all. The exclusion is gently painful, but it is enough to see them, to watch them grow.

They grow rapidly. The dark of their faces shrinks to two smuts either side of their noses. The orange fur begins to smoulder. Their ears become disproportionate. They are quick, ridiculously clumsy, unable to control their energy. He laughs, for the first time in months. Then their play turns savage, tumbling and biting. They learn to focus, peering at small moving quarry; they stalk, chew beetles, snap at airborne insects, while their mother lies in the grass, exhausted by them. She brings fresh carcasses, which they tug at, shaking their heads, twisting off strips of carrion. And still she feeds them her milk, though they are two-thirds her size and he can see the discomfort of her being emptied, of manufacturing and lending nutrients. Sometimes she looks at him, as if waiting for his decision.

He is a man with two lives. He works, he holds conversations with office staff, shops at the supermarket. He turns down dates, but seems contented, and his colleagues wonder if he has, without declaration, moved on. Esmé is re-employed, though she is sad Sophia Garnett has left her husband and suspects injustice against her to be the cause – whatever that may be. But she finds no trace of any other woman in the house, no lace underwear, no lost earring or hairs gathered in the sink. He watches men lifting their children out of car seats and up from toppled bicycles. If anyone were to ask, he would say, *I am not without happiness.*

He walks the heath. He monitors the landscape. He worries about the cubs, the multitude of dangers, even as they grow larger and stronger, and he can see all that they will be. They ambush their mother, who at times seems sallow, having sacrificed her quota of prey, having no mate to help her. They show interest in the rubbish of the woods, bringing back wrappers and foil, even the arm of a plastic doll. There will be dispersal, he knows, but not yet. For now, they are hers, and perhaps his, though peripherally. One day an idea strikes him. He goes to the den site. They are not there, but he doesn't linger. He takes from his pocket the little purple ball Sophia used to keep in her purse. He places it by the entrance. The next time he comes it has vanished. He looks around until he finds it, lying under a thornbush nearby. He picks it up. There are teethmarks in the surface, scratches, signs of play.

What will become of them he does not

know. The woods are temporary and the city is rapacious. He has given up looking for meaning. Why is a useless question, an unknowable object. But to suspend thought is impossible. The mind is made perfectly of possibilities. One day, Sophia might walk through the garden, naked, her hair long and tangled, her body gloried by use. She will open the back door, which is never locked, and enter the kitchen and sit at the table. *I dreamt of the forest again*, she will say.

It is a forgivable romance, high conceit – he knows. At night he lies in bed, not at its centre, but closer to the midway point. He thinks of Sophia, whom he loved. He no more expects her to return than he conceived of her departure. But he imagines her stepping across the room, bare, and damp from the shower. And then he thinks of the fox, in her blaze, in her magnificence. It is she who quarters his mind, she whose absence strikes fear into his heart. Her loss would be unendurable. To watch her run into the edgelands, breasting the ferns and scorching the fields, to see her disappear into the void –

how could life mean anything without his unbelonging wife?

ff

Haweswater

Winner of the Commonwealth Writers' Prize

It is 1936 in a remote dale in the old, north-ern county of Westmorland. When a man from Manchester arrives, spokesman for a vast industrial project to create a new reser-voir, the villagers must come to terms with the fact that this corner of Lakeland will be transformed. Jack Liggett, the Waterworks representative, begins a troubled and intense affair with Janet Lightburn from the village. A woman of force and strength of mind, her natural orthodoxy deeply influences him. Finally, in tragic circumstances, a remark-able, desperate act on Janet's part attempts to restore the valley to its former state.

'Strikingly original.' Margaret Forster

Available in paperback and ebook now

ff

The Electric Michelangelo

Shortlisted for the MAN Booker Prize

On the windswept front of Morecambe Bay, Cy Parks spends his childhood years first in a guest house for consumptives run by his mother and then as apprentice to alcoholic tattoo artist Eliot Riley. Thirsty for new experiences, he departs for America and finds himself in the riotous world of the Coney Island boardwalk, where he sets up his own business as 'The Electric Michelangelo'. In this carnival environment of roller-coasters and freak-shows, Cy becomes enamoured with Grace, a mysterious immigrant and circus performer who commissions him to cover her entire body in tattooed eyes.

'Hugely atmospheric.' *Independent*

Available in paperback and ebook now

ff

The Carhullan Army

Winner of the John Llewellyn Rhys Prize

Jackie and a group of fellow rebel women have escaped the Authority's repressive regime, forming a militia in the far north of Cumbria. Sister, brought to breaking point by the restrictions imposed on her own life, decides to join them. Though her journey is frightening and dangerous, she believes her struggle will soon be over. But Jackie's single-minded vision for the army means that Sister must decide all over again what freedom is, and whether she is willing to fight for it.

'As rich and exhilarating as it is disturbing.' *The Times*

Available in paperback and ebook now